Stop .. Bobby!

Written by Miriam Simon

Illustrated by Julie Park

Rosie made a hedgehog.

Bobby squashed it.

'Stop it, Bobby!' said Rosie.

But Bobby didn't stop it.

3

Sam made a fox.

Bobby squashed it.

'Stop it, Bobby!' said Sam.

But Bobby didn't stop it.

4

He took Tilak's book.

'Stop it, Bobby!' said Tilak.

Then Bobby took Mo's book.
'Stop it, Bobby!' shouted Mo,
and she hit him.

Mrs Hall said, 'Stop it, Mo.'
Mo said, 'He took my book.'

Mrs Hall said, 'Stop it, Bobby.'

At playtime, Sam and Rosie and
Mo and Tilak played football.

Bobby wanted to play but
Mo said, 'No!'

Bobby took the ball.

'Stop it!' said Tilak.

But Bobby didn't stop it.

He kicked the ball on the roof.

Then he ran away.

'You can't stop me,' he shouted.

'You can't stop me!'

Bang!

He ran into the wall.

He hurt his hand and he hurt his
knee and he cried.

Sam ran to Bobby and
Rosie ran to Mrs Hall.
She shouted, 'Bobby's hurt his hand
and he's hurt his knee.'

15

Mrs Hall put a plaster on Bobby's knee.

Then Rosie said, 'He took our ball.'

Mrs Hall looked at Bobby and
Bobby said, 'Sorry.'

17

Bobby wanted to make a hedgehog.

Rosie helped him.

Sam helped him too.

Bobby made a hedgehog . . .